Mini Sagas

Mini Marvels

SURREY

First published in Great Britain in 2010 by
Young Writers, Remus House, Coltsfoot Drive,
Peterborough, PE2 9JX
Tel (01733) 890066 Fax (01733) 313524
Website: www.youngwriters.co.uk

Disclaimer
Young Writers has maintained every effort
to publish stories that will not cause offence.
Any stories, events or activities relating to individuals
should be read as fictional pieces and not construed
as real-life character portrayal.

Design by Spencer Hart

Foreword

Since Young Writers was established in 1990, our aim has been to promote and encourage written creativity amongst children and young adults. By giving aspiring young authors the chance to be published, Young Writers effectively nurtures the creative talents of the next generation, allowing their confidence and writing ability to grow.

With our latest fun competition, *The Adventure Starts Here ...* , secondary school children nationwide were given the tricky challenge of writing a story with a beginning, middle and an end in just fifty words.

The diverse and imaginative range of entries made the selection process a difficult but enjoyable task with stories chosen on the basis of style, expression, flair and technical skill. A fascinating glimpse into the imaginations of the future, we hope you will agree that this entertaining collection is one that will amuse and inspire the whole family.

Contents

Grey Court School

Howard of Effingham School

The Mini Sagas

Second Life

Absentmindedly, Jack walked down to the park.
He hated TV. He loved to play board games. He
loved Monopoly; Death Monopoly. He needed
to find the swings. He must roll the dice. They
felt heavy in his pocket. He swung high, falling …
thud! The game was over.
He woke up.

Luciano Simeon (12)

The Getaway

One day I saw an old man in a scary building near my convenience store kicking up the juice cartons in his worn out old shoes. Then he chased me down the street kicking up the papers. I turned and punched the old man. He fell; I ran.

Joe Hall (14)
Bensham Manor School

Big Momma

There was once a man who called himself Big Momma. He liked to dress up as a big funny woman.
One day he was running to the beach and he fell over. A lady helped him up, they fell in love and had five kids.

Victoria Maynard (14)
Bensham Manor School

3

The Note

I was working on my coursework when a boy came in. Everybody stared. He gave a slip to Miss. Everybody was quiet. The slip said, 'Go home', but didn't give a reason. I was worried, a horrid feeling hit me. I got home. A note said, 'Dentist'. Relieved, I remembered.

Teagan Bransome (14)
Farnham Heath End School

Ghost In The Vicinity

Creak. 'Argh! That creaking's freaking me out,' said Cody.
'I know,' said John. A vase clattered to the floor into minuscule pieces. The poltergeist was in the vicinity. The curtains swayed to and fro. Their souls were stolen. The ghost moved on to the next unsuspecting, endangered victims.
Good luck!

Ryan Larby (13)
Farnham Heath End School

5

Horror Of Humpty

Humpty sat on a wall. Suddenly Humpty had
a huge fall because of a flock of bananas that
attacked poor Humpty! All of the ghosts and the
ghosts' knights couldn't help Humpty with all of
their might. All of the ghosts crawled down a well
and slowly eroded into Hell.

Mason King (14)
Farnham Heath End School

The Pied Piper Of Hamelin

'How are we going to get rid of the rats?' Bob
asked. A man burst into the room.
'I will!' he exclaimed.
'How?' the town council asked.
'Watch me.'
Days later the rats had disappeared. Disputes
about the man's pay made him abduct
everybody's children. They were never seen
again.

James Traylen (13)
Farnham Heath End School

7

Humpty Dumpty's Fall

Humpty Dumpty sat on the wall, Humpty
Dumpty had a great fall. All the king's horses and
all the king's men, *could* put Humpty together
again. All thanks to this country's amazing NHS
workers, who worked tirelessly for Humpty
Dumpty's needs.
Gosh I love this beautiful and brilliant country!

James Asker (13)

Farnham Heath End School

8

Perfect

Tuesday had loved Sebastian as long as she could remember. He was clever, kind, funny, and there he was, just a few inches from her, his brilliant brown eyes boring into hers. Without thinking, she leaned forwards, and their lips met. It was the most glorious moment in Tuesday's life.

Annie Farthing (13)
Farnham Heath End School

9

Untitled

Clutching a chocolate bar in his sweaty palms,
he realised he didn't have enough money.
Without thinking he shoved it in his pocket and
ran towards the door, but then a massive hand
grabbed him. 'Where do you think you're going?'
a rough voice boomed in his ear.

Gigi Douglas-Hiley (12)
Frensham Heights School

Untitled

Falling, falling … A tear trickled down her rose-red cheek. She could hear voices of the scared, screaming in peril. Still falling towards the edge she could see a flickering light coming towards her. A child was running screaming, 'Don't die now!' It sped to her. Coming, then it hit.

Kwabena Osae-Addo (12)
Frensham Heights School

Drowning

I gasped for air as I reached the surface. Then *crash!* Another wave tugged me under. I was swimming. There was a current, it had dragged me out to the rocks. Now I was fighting for my life. I surfaced again only to be pulled under for the last time.

Isobel Carlill (12)
Frensham Heights School

Hope

I was in the room, alone. I heard another window shatter. It echoed through me. A shiver ran down my spine. I kept quiet, hiding in the darkness. I could hear the sound of my heart beating against my chest. In the distance the approaching police sirens gave me hope …

Alana Boden (12)
Frensham Heights School

The Heist

New York City, rush hour, a gang of masked robbers hurry out of a high-rise building, climb into a red sports car. They zoom into the traffic hotly pursued by police. They race through the city, causing havoc and crashes. The police smash into a lorry, the robbers escape.

Ben Acton (12)

Frensham Heights School

The Snow Queen

Once there was a beautiful queen with skin as
white as snow. She had two daughters.
One day the queen was telling the story about the
green man. She kissed them goodnight and went
to leave the room. Then suddenly she fell to the
ground. Dead, silent and stone cold.

Annie Handscomb (13)
Frensham Heights School

15

The Voice

My mind was captured by the mysterious sound.
It would speak to me. I would listen. 'Help me,'
it would call. 'Follow me.' I would always be
restrained, one way or another. It kept on calling
and one day I followed. Why did I follow? And I
never came back.

Olivia Perl (12)
Frensham Heights School

Light

Emerging from unconsciousness I'm aware that something is wrong. I feel painless, light-headed. My eyelids flicker open but my searching eyes can only find blackness. I spin around frantically, feeling suddenly claustrophobic. My eyes settle on a prick of light. It enlarges quickly and engulfs me. Death takes me.

Anna David (12)

Frensham Heights School

Halfway Up The Mountain

I was halfway up the mountain. I had a way to go.
It started to get icy but I was a good climber and
had lots of practise so I was not worried. Then I
tripped and fell down. I hit my head and I never
ever woke up.

William Christie (12)
Frensham Heights School

Christmas Time

It was the night before Christmas. I was really
excited about getting all my presents. I stayed up
all night. 1 o'clock, 2 o'clock, 3 o'clock, 4 o'clock,
and all through the night o'clock. I was so very
bored.
When I woke up it was the 9th of March!

Dan Cooper (13)
Frensham Heights School

19

The Three Little Pigs And The Cooker

Three little pigs were annoyed by a wolf. The first pig wanted to shoot him but shot himself by accident. The second pig wanted to feed him to a bear but shut himself in the cage. The last pig decided to cook him which succeeded and he ate the remains.

Edward Hammonds (12)

Frensham Heights School

Forever Alone

She sat in the corner, on her own, no one to talk to. No one knew her, no one wanted to. We heard a scream, we ran outside. She was lying on the road, blood dripping from her mouth, eyes rolled into the back of her head. It fell silent.

Saskia Hardcastle (12)
Frensham Heights School

Little Did We Know

We were running with happiness, ready to start a new life in a different country. Little did we know what was about to happen. As we checked into the airport we felt the ground rumble and shake below us. It was an earthquake. We all screamed. We all fell silent.

Saraya Haddad (12)
Frensham Heights School

The Life Of A Peruvian Guinea Pig

Life was good. Every day we got grass.
Sometimes people would leave, I did not know
why. Then I left, it was very strange. Soon a hand
went around my head and a vigorous movement
was made. Before I knew it I was a kebab and
that was the end.

Dean Abele (13)
Frensham Heights School

23

Pedro

Once there was a taco called Pedro Sombrero,
living in a shop window. He dreamed of
performing on a Broadway stage, dancing for all
his adoring fans.

One day, someone bought him. *'Nooooo!'*
Pedro yodelled; and from then on, he became a
Broadway success as the first ever yodelling taco.

Mylo McDonald (13)
Frensham Heights School

All That's Left Is A Pair Of Scissors And A Blood-soaked Tissue

She sat in the corner staring at the floor …
On her way home that evening it was so dark and
cold. She was crossing the road, there was a car
with no lights on, he didn't see her. That was the
last time we saw that girl in the corner.

Ellie Brown (12)
Frensham Heights School

Attentio Deficit

'I will just get my handbag! Stay here!' She got out of the car and ran into the house, the phone rang. 'Hello?' Unaware of her children making their steady descent down the drive, tapping at the window shouting her name. She had left the handbrake off! *Squeak! Bang!* 'Kids?'

Isabel Watts (12)

Frensham Heights School

Untitled

Walk in, the doorbell rings. They all look at me,
see right through me. I sit down, fear takes over,
knees trembling. They read out my name. I walk
in, I lay on the bed. A man in a white coat reaches
for tweezers. 'This won't hurt a bit.'

Dylan Willis (13)
Frensham Heights School

Running

Running, heart pounding. I could hear footsteps coming closer. Stomach churning, legs numb and throbbing. I could not carry on any longer. Bloodshot eyes flooded with tears. I started to stumble as I panicked even more. Suddenly I felt the cold and hard floor on my cheek. I had collapsed.

Does Moolenaar (12)
Frensham Heights School

My Friend's Imaginary Friend

My friend's imaginary friend is an elf called
Flibboo. He dances about and plays ping-pong
against my friend's head. My friend says this is
why he gets migraines. My friend's mum says he
is crazy and that he needs to go to the doctor. I've
never seen him again.

Tom Baron (12)
Frensham Heights School

29

Moonlight

The eyes appeared out of the gloom with malicious looks. Trees whistled with delight. The eyes came closer, revealing bloodstained teeth. Growling erupted in the dark. The moon illuminated the ground. Then I saw the loose flesh and guts littered across the floor. The moon had shown me the outcome.

Freddie Carleton-Smith (12)

Frensham Heights School

King Of The Jungle

Ironic, is it not? I, the king of Africa decorate
Man's floor. Blackened by shoes and worn by feet.
I remember chasing them over the Savannah,
I the predator, they my prey. But times have
changed. Now I'm not worth the dust from their
feet. Pathetic old hearth rug.

Sophie Sinclair-Brown
Fullbrook School

31

The Three Pigs Revisited

As the three pigs ran into the house made of sticks, the wolf chased after them. 'I'll blow your house down!' cried the wolf but these sticks were reinforced and Wolfie couldn't blow them down! So he got an industrial steamroller and ploughed the place down. Didn't pig guts fly!

Dan Punter (14)

Fullbrook School

White-Coated Monsters

The white-coated monsters wailed, hiding behind laminated doors with sharp steel weapons and icy cold hands. Sweat dripped down my forehead as I waited, my friends one by one forced into their torture chambers. They called my name and I froze. 'Ready for your flu jab?'

Abby McPhail (15)
Fullbrook School

The Torture Chamber

Dragged into the torture chamber by my legs
and arms, I struggled as they tried to lift me onto
the deathbed, strapping me down. Suddenly
a buzzing sound, coming towards me as the
masked shadow approached. 'Nooo!' I screamed.
I tried to get loose but nothing was working. The
dentist!

Nuzhat Ali (14)
Fullbrook School

Feasting On My Fear

I took a deep breath and opened the door. The sun was glistening menacingly on the weapons, their sharp points feasting on my fear. I could feel my heart pounding faster, faster. Sweat dripped down my temple. My hands clammy. I stopped. 'So, just a filling today, Miss Marsh?'

Lily Pettett (14)
Fullbrook School

35

Untitled

The house was pitch-black when Niamh found her parents lying unconscious on their bed. She ran to grab the phone but the phone was floating in mid-air. She ran away only to find she couldn't get out. Then she saw her parents and they yelled, 'April Fools!'

Chloe Lowe-Hagan (11)

Grey Court School

Melon

Once there was a magic, mystical, mysterious
melon that could walk and he lived in Melonland.
But the cruel, crazy carrot wanted to kill him
so the mystical melon was forced to move to
England and was never seen in Melonland ever
again. Unfortunately he was splattered by a car.

Hugo Russell (12)
Grey Court School

37

It!

Sera didn't know what it was till it was too late …
Only this morning she felt on top of the world.
But when she got home she was in for a surprise.
By the time she got to bed her fate was sealed!
She saw it … What could it be?

Luke Hunter (12)
Grey Court School

John And Bob's Lovely Treasure

John and Bob were two colossal crooks.
One day they decided to put their past behind
them.
They both went to Egypt one day to find the
treasure hidden by their great grandad. In the end
they both found the hidden treasure, a golden
medallion, colossal money and more!

Olalekan Akinbam (12)

Grey Court School

The Three Little Wolves

Three wolves lived in houses of straw, wood and brick. A bad pig came to the straw house and oinked it down. The wolf ran to the next house, so did the other wolf. The pig tried to oink it down but it could not!

Lauren Mcivor-Main (12)

Grey Court School

40

My First Day At My New School

As I arrived at my new school I waved goodbye to
my mum but I felt scared which made me queasy.
As I walked into my new class everybody stared
and glared with fear. Then I saw my friends who
started to cheer, but I was trembling with fear.

Melissa Jassar (12)
Grey Court School

Strangers In The House

Knock, knock! Jeff went to open the door but there was no one there. 'That's strange,' he said. Suddenly the fridge door slammed shut. 'Mum? Dad?' Jeff called. 'Are you there?' No answer. All of a sudden someone (no, something) grabbed him from behind.

'Happy birthday!' shouted the whole family.

Ben Kelly (13)
Grey Court School

Mist

As mist settled over the Mystical Moors, I became
aware I was not the only one on the moors.
I turned around, but there was no one there.
Then I heard a raspy breathing right behind me.
'Is anybody there?' I called out. I spun around. I
screamed and ran.

Henry Teague (12)
Grey Court School

43

The Giant Of Sparta

One day in Sparta there was a small village but they had a problem. There was a mighty giant who demanded one live body to feast on every week. They sent a diseased pig dressed as a man. The giant ate it and died. The village was at last free!

Lloyd Alfie Nellis (12)
Grey Court School

Dead!

Alice was alone. She was walking through an alleyway at night. She turned around. There was a figure not ten paces away. She heard a click of a gun getting ready to fire. In his arms was her little sister. 'Turn around,' said the figure. *Bang!* Her body fell. Dead ...

Ruby Scutter (11)
Grey Court School

Cindy And The Seven Evil Dwarves

The witch glared in the mirror. Cindy was
sweeping gardens. 'Who is the fairest of all?' the
witch screamed.
'Cindy!' replied the mirror. Cindy was banished
into the woods. She found a grotty house and
seven dwarves. They gnarled, sank their teeth
into her and feasted on her cold flesh!

Summer Gedall (11)

Grey Court School

Death

I came home from school and the moment I stepped through the door I knew something was wrong. The house was empty and there was a strange dripping sound, which was weird because the plumber had turned off our water. I walked upstairs and saw my loving parents, dead.

Dominic Kelly (13)
Grey Court School

The Clatter On The Roof

It was a crisp, cold Christmas Eve. A young,
clumsy child, very excited, drifted off to sleep
so slowly. During the night there was a clatter.
She crept out of her room, down the stairs.
Something was rustling under the tree. 'Hello?'
she whispered.
'Ho! Ho! Ho!' he replied.

Thomas Steward (12)
Grey Court School

Dead Love

Sarah stood over the stone grave, weeping at
the loss of her vampire husband, Daniel. As she
put the bouquet of roses down on the grave
and walked away a hand grabbed her ankle! She
screamed at the horror! She turned, looked
down, seeing Daniel rising up from the ground …

Maisie Robinson (12)

Grey Court School

A Bad Holiday!

'We won!' yelled Alice. The Page family had won a trip to Park Island.

Next day they went to the airport. When they got to the island there was no hotel, they were abandoned. They spent days and nights on the island when suddenly one night a boat finally came!

Miarah Lucas (11)

Grey Court School

The Car Broke down

We were on a motorway, our car had broken
down. Max went to get petrol. I turned on the
radio for comfort. A psychopath was on the
loose. I was worried, Max had been out for ages.
Thump! Blood gushed down the windscreen!
Max's head rolled down the windscreen. 'Argh!'

Amber Dass-Peacock (11)
Grey Court School

Death By Night

It was cold and the world seemed to die. I went down an alleyway. Something was creeping up my back. I turned to see an alien, green and slimy, stopping my heart. It started to devour me, ripping my flesh and gobbling me up. It was the end.

Mazhar Choudhry (12)

Grey Court School

Thump

Jack was scared. The alley was filled with shadows. He sprinted! He turned around. A demon! Red with horns and fiery eyes! It seemed to appear out of thin air! *Thump!* The floor was moving against him! Pulling him back! The demon came closer! *Thump!* Silence. He turned around! *Thump!*

Jad Steel (11)
Grey Court School

Untitled

Chloe came home to find that the house was empty and that the lights weren't working. *It's 4.30. Mum and Dad are meant to be back. Where are they?* she thought. She could hear voices coming from upstairs so Chloe made her way up. No one was there.

Niamh-Hannah Brown (11)

Grey Court School

The Despairing Dead

Nick just left. I would have said something but the tears welled up in my eyes so I just dropped the flowers and cried. Then I felt a bony hand tighten on my shoulder, it dragged me down into a grave. I screamed but it was in vain, I fainted.

Jack Haughton (12)

Grey Court School

55

The Orphan Killer

Sam was an orphan, he'd just moved into a horrible, horrific, ghastly house. He was unloved and hated.

That night he was attacked by his foster family. He killed them with his knife and ran from the police.

They're still chasing him. No one knows why he killed the family.

Tom Benefield (11)
Grey Court School

The Shoe That Went To Iraq

Shoe was in a Ferrari Enzo in Iraq. A missile
nearly hit Shoe. He revved the engine. He
travelled at 205mph. Then a soldier jumped on
Shoe's car and tried to get in but Shoe stopped
him. The soldier had a bomb so blew up the car.
Boooom!

Mohamed Redaoui (12)

Grey Court School

57

Captured

As the blackness crept up on the cloudy grey sky, the trees became silhouettes against the navy sky. She ran. They were after her and their loud footsteps were drawing closer. She tripped! Darkness. They had captured her. No escape.

Ellie Byrne (14)
Howard of Effingham School

The Broken Silence

Gunshots echoed behind Dan as he frantically negotiated the matted roots that made up the swamp. As bullets whistled past him, Dan drew his own sleek wooden-handled pistol and began to fire back. *Thump!* As Dan picked himself up he was met by the unmistakable stare of a pistol …

Luke Brunswick (13)
Howard of Effingham School

59

How To Ruin An Expensive Jacket

The blade hung by a single string above its victim. The cord was cut, the menacing blade of the guillotine ready to chew into flesh. Metal sunk through the throat, slicing cleanly. Death came instantly, biting through. The executioner was pleased, he glanced down. Blood doesn't wash off silk.

William Hughes (13)
Howard of Effingham School

Substitute Teacher

The stressed substitute teacher called repeatedly
for silence but each attempt made no effect on
the rowdy children, lounging carelessly on desks,
calling out the window, texting their friends
and bragging about their laptops. Enter the
headmaster and students suddenly paused and sat
as if nothing bad ever happened. Silence.

Rachel Stanley (13)
Howard of Effingham School

The Storm

The hard rain battered the roof. Endless noise, endless sorrow. The pain of the last few years was pouring out. Tears flooded down her cheek like waterfalls over a chasm. How did it come to this? Why her? The door smashed open. The storm swept her away. Gone. Forever.

Aron White (13)
Howard of Effingham School

The End Of The Abyss

The end was in sight, looking round I saw no sign
of the creature. I dragged my feet, step by step,
but as I got closer the end seemed further away.
Time was ticking, there was nowhere to run,
nowhere to hide, nowhere to go, backwards or
forwards …

Maddy Clark (13)
Howard of Effingham School

63

A Melting Moment

Words hit Alice like freezing icicles, crushing her body. She seemed alone in this world, nobody to trust. Her feet felt as if they were rooted to the pavement. She knew if she ran, they would follow. Unexpectedly warm words flowed towards her, encouraging her to join them. Alice smiled!

Charlotte Bird (13)

Howard of Effingham School

Untitled

A pair of bright topaz eyes stared at her from the end of the room, like liquid gold. Her feet cemented to the floor. Her scream locked in her throat. Why? From across the room the figure clicked his fingers. The sound echoed in her mind, darkness filled her head.

Ruth Harrison (13)

Howard of Effingham School

65

The Cold Veil

Sound erupts around me. Shrapnel rains down. Hard cold steel settles against the chaotic landscape. A blood-red sky marks the horror that's been witnessed. The despair and destruction. Not buildings but families. Torn apart, separated by the cold veil of death. The veil that has left me … all alone.

Laura Richards (13)
Howard of Effingham School

66

50 Words?

'How many?' cried Bill. 'Exactly 50?' *This is going to be hard,* Bill thought. All of a sudden he had it. A masterpiece. Bill grinned from ear to ear as he checked his work. A sudden smile turned to a frown, his gleam went to tears. 'No! Only 49 words!'

George Bishop (14)
Howard of Effingham School

67

How Hard Is It To Drink?

Surely it's not that hard for people to drink from a cup. Fill it with whatever you want. Then put it on your mouth and tip, but it's not that easy for me. Do you know why? I have drinking problems. Oops. Better get changed and try again.

Ellen Phillpot (12)
Howard of Effingham School

Daisy And The Pigeon

I see fresh grass so I waddle down the stairs and
run out and go to my favourite place. I see an
intruder pigeon! I charge at it, bite at its feathers
and run at it. It is very fun showing who's boss.
Finally I can enjoy my grass.

Anna Monk (11)
Howard of Effingham School

The Vampire

I saw his beautiful marble-like face and fell in love. He just sat there like a statue. He didn't eat, he didn't drink. I was staring at him then in a blink of an eye he was gone. I looked to my side and he was right there.

Amy Jennings (12)
Howard of Effingham School

Gates Of Hell

'Caught here in a fiery blaze. Won't lose my will
to stay.'
'Boiling hot weather, a barren empty sight.'
'Mental fiction follows me, show me what it's like
to be set free ... '
'As the gates of Hell open, all comes clear,
demons shall have their day ... today.'
'Critical acclaim ... thirteen.'

Aston O'Shaughnessy (13)
Howard of Effingham School

71

I Hate Cars And Rain

6am. I hate car journeys. I hate rain. I'm in a car
and it's raining. I'm bored.
6.01am. I'm bored. It's gonna be very hot when
we get there. Mum said so.
7.02am. I'm still bored.
9.30am. Still mega bored, bored.
5pm. Hoorah we're there.
5.01pm. It's raining.

Katie McClung (12)
Howard of Effingham School

My Chocolate Coin

I'll buy, I'll buy a chocolate coin. Oh wait, oh wait,
it's not enough. I'll go, I'll go and buy another one.
Hang on a second that's still not enough. I start
chewing another one when I realise I am sitting in
class chewing the end of my pencil.

Katy Ranger (11)
Howard of Effingham School

The Black Death

The Black Death struck England from 1348-1350.
It was a horrible disease, people stuck chicken
bottoms or frog legs under their arms. Most
people died from the disease, about 50% died.
They got lumps under the arms called buboes
that had a horrible black puss inside.

Jessica Birks (11)
Howard of Effingham School

Untitled

We have lost contact with our agents. We need
to secure safe passage for the Queen. We need to
recruit some new agents, ones with much more
skill, smart, leadership skills, co-operation and
they need to look like they are part of the crowd.
We need some children.

Daniel Moore (11)
Howard of Effingham School

75

Lucky Them!

As they both stumbled off to the plane I was the one who had to be stuck with the cat whose fluff always trailed around. There was also Katy my babysitter who I thought was very strange. I stumbled off to sulk. 'They always go on holiday. Lucky them!'

Niamh Clarke (11)
Howard of Effingham School

A Caring Friend

She's gone. My eyes flood up. Shivers run down
my spine. I'm alone. I'm soaking wet. Water
seeps through the holes in my shoes. I'm down,
depressed. When suddenly a touch of warmth
slips through my fingers. The whole world sparks
up. Someone's there, someone cares. They're
there for me.

Kate Roberts (12)
Howard of Effingham School

See You Tonight

31 October '09.
Went to a movie with a mate. It was called
'See You Tonight!' Sounds scary but was so
not. Needed the toilet on the way, we saw a
ghost! We went into the toilet, came out. It
was members of staff tricking people; it was
Hallowe'en!

Aseya Ali (11)
Howard of Effingham School

Reading Before Sleeping

I watch TV until 9 o'clock at night then trudge
upstairs to my totally untidy room. I put on my
pyjamas and read until my mum comes up and
tells me to stop. When she is in bed I continue
reading but every time she tells me to stop,
continuously!

James Smith (12)
Howard of Effingham School

The Zombie Slayer

Zombies were all around me. I leaped into the air dramatically and landed, thundering a powerful shockwave, slaughtering the dead. An incredible screech flew me back, the leader was there! I charged forth with intense focus …
My mum sighed. She'd never approved of me playing so many video games.

Callum London (11)
Howard of Effingham School

Lights

Jab. Jab. Falling. *Smash.* People hurrying, shouting urgently, where am I? Someone's holding my hand. I hear my name. Open eyes. Can't. Say something. Can't. Move. Can't. I hear church bells, a choir singing. Such sweet heavenly sounds. I see a light, so bright. Is this my way back home?

Lucy Meadows (12)
Howard of Effingham School

81

Untitled

One day me and Megan went to Epsom. When we got there we went into a shop and tried some high heels on. We were in the changing rooms and then we both fell over because the heels were too high! We burst out laughing.

Amy Farrer (12)
Howard of Effingham School

Worried About Nothing

Sitting in classroom, eating Skittles with friend.
Watching out for teachers. Letting guard down
and relaxing; taking another sweet. Finishing
packet, opening another. Teacher walks in, not
noticing us. Teacher looks up, sees us frozen,
eating sweets. Teacher sits down next to us.
Sitting in classroom, eating Skittles with teacher.

Ellen Knight (11)
Howard of Effingham School

Up

Carl and Ellie had a dream to fly to Paradise Falls.
They got married and one day would fly there
together.
After many years of happy life Ellie died of old
age.
Years later Carl set off on his adventure, when
suddenly there was a knock on the door …

Amelia Judd (11)
Howard of Effingham School

A Mouse In My Mouth

I wander around with a mouse in my mouth.
Stopping it wriggling away. I can't put it down. It's
way too risky. I have to take its life. I rip off its
head. What a delight. I've never tried it before.
Leave the body there. The humans won't care.
Hopefully.

Frank Smith (11)
Howard of Effingham School

85

Mother!

It was Tuesday night and it was the day I was dreaming would never come. It was my mum, she was in hospital. I was scared. What would happen? I loved her, I needed her, I wanted her … She finally came home!

Chloe Lansdell (11)
Howard of Effingham School

A Moment Of Moonlight

She jumped, deep into the blue. A force within her was pulling, leading the way. Searching, searching for something; not knowing. Through an arch it led her. Forward, forward to a pool. A pool of magic. The moon came overhead. Flash, translucent white legs transformed. Behind, a tail.

Rhiannon Pither (14)
Howard of Effingham School

Here It Comes Again!

There I lay, awake. For I had been asleep. A squeak in the room got me up like a bolt, my tired eyes adjusting to the room surrounding my weak, unprotected body. A cloak of darkness covering my eyes. A burglar, a murderer? Wait … there it was again!

James Lambert (13)
Howard of Effingham School

Stranger

One wise and one foolish woman travel by night.
They meet a pale, handsome stranger, with
glowing eyes, needle-sharp teeth. He invites
them to his home, a majestic castle. One woman,
blinded by his wealth and beauty accepts. The
other declines. She will never see her foolish
friend again.

Emma Mackintosh (14)
Howard of Effingham School

The Pit

Here I am once again, lying in the pit, cuts and drips of blood streaming down my acne-ridden face, the face that got me here in the first place. Children and teachers watch and stare, just waiting for me to cry. Bullies ruin my life, just for fun.

Miles Burton (13)

Howard of Effingham School

Neek

They call her 'Neek'. Make-up isn't slathered
over her face. She doesn't wear the 'right'
clothes, say the 'right' things. She's in the top sets.
Conscientiousness leaks from her; whilst anger
bubbles explosively deep inside. Every day she
suffers in silence but never underestimate the
quiet face of revenge.

Imogen Morris (13)
Howard of Effingham School

Watch The Cookie

Watch the cookie cook in the oven, every second getting longer. It's done, yes! Don't care if it's hot, can't wait much longer. Put the choc chip cookie in my mouth. I knew waiting all that time wasn't worth it. Now only 8 more! Yuck, yuck, yuck. That was horrid!

Hamish Clifford (11)
Howard of Effingham School

The Flying Balloon

Wow! I love being a balloon, flying high, I feel like I
own everything when I'm watching the sky. Birds
look at me in complete awe, but me, no thoughts,
just flying high. Oh no! What's that? A bird or not?
Argh! It's an aeroplane. The end … of me!

Nadia Peppard (12)
Howard of Effingham School

93

Life Of A Butterfly

I open my eyes, fresh flowers all around me.
Stretch, it feels so good to be free. One, two,
three, jump in the sky. I reach for the moon, I
can go so high. I see what I'm looking for down
below, land softly, head high, my wings on show.

Annabel Blythe
Howard of Effingham School

94

My Best Friend

I was talking to my best friend, it was amazing.
I said that I loved her as much as anything in
the whole entire world. She was my best friend
because she was always there for me. Then I
found out that I was just looking in the mirror.
'Argh!'

Victoria Goodall (12)
Howard of Effingham School

95

Blood In Volterra

There was no warning. It came, like most other
things: unexpectedly. We didn't understand
at first, but within an instant, we realised
simultaneously what was happening. It was
already too late, nothing could possibly save us all.
The first victim was taken: his blood stained the
walls. It was Death.

Amy Martin (14)
Howard of Effingham School

Doggy Gunner

There was a posh family who had a dog. An evil
vet came round and took the dog back to his
house. The vet used to be in the army and had
lots of guns so the dog shot the vet.

Joe Jackson (11)
Howard of Effingham School

97

Cycling

Cycling - it is my first time. I feel on top of the world. I say, 'I am doing it!' My mum and dad are so pleased. I am going really fast but I can't stop. The next thing I know I am in a hedge. I've learned how to brake!

Sam Judd (11)

Howard of Effingham School

Hello, Goodbye

Hello, goodbye. You have to say these words:
hello, goodbye. You have to say them both at
least once a day.
Here I go again as the phone rings, 'Hello …
goodbye.' As I say it, it happens again and again to
people all over the world.
Hello, goodbye.

Matthew Goodwin (12)
Howard of Effingham School

Untitled

I am walking, I am walking, I see a dog. I am
walking, I am walking, I see a clown. I am walking,
I am walking, I see a zombie. Oh wait, oh wait, I'd
better run …
Oh it's just my mum waking me up!

Lucy Mathias (11)
Howard of Effingham School

Mother

1901.
Dear Mother, I hate this school. I'm really hating
it. Take me home, Bobita.
Dear Bobita, put a sock in it, Mum.
1971.
Dear Bobita, wheeze ... cough ... help please,
Mum.
Dear Mother, maybe later.

Jack Sutherland
Howard of Effingham School

101

The Escape

Finally, we got to the stairs but my lace was caught. With Jim right behind me, we both tumbled down the stairs. Not stopping to look at our cuts and bruises, we jumped up and dived through the window.

Chris Martin (11)

Howard of Effingham School

Fly, Fly, Fly Away

My life starts as a block of rubbery rubber. I am melted and shaped. I am very small but I can stretch and become quite big. I can be filled with a very thin gas, after this I can fly. I can fly and fly and fly! Then *pop!*

Theo Gembler (12)

Howard of Effingham School

The Poor Dragon

There was a princess named Mia. She went on a stroll through the enchanted forest. Suddenly a purple dragon leaped at her. It roared. A superhero flew down to help Mia, she thought. But no. He took the dragon. He was more scared of her than she was of him!

Jake Berryman (12)
Howard of Effingham School

Homework Time

Sitting down at the desk, pen in hand, sheet of paper before me. I started writing. This was amazing, exhilarating, astounding and exciting. I looked down at what I had written. 'Once'. I sighed, feeling my afternoon slipping away like Mercury. One word down, only 9999 words to go. Damn.

Alastair Reher
Howard of Effingham School

Don't Go To Jail

Oh yes, oh yes. I am so cool. I robbed the
jewellery shop, I can afford a swimming pool!
I have a billion pounds, I can afford a trillion
clowns! Oh dear, oh dear, I am in jail. I am the
worst and biggest fail.

Matthew Cole (11)
Howard of Effingham School

A Day As A Ball

'Ow, oh ow! What was that for? Will you just
stop? Being a ball really hurts! Everywhere you
go, you just get kicked, punched or generally,
disfigured. It's a penalty so I've got to gooooo …
'Score!' shouts the commentator.

Bill Walker-Trivett (13)
Howard of Effingham School

The Day In The Life Of A Coke Can

He takes one look at me. Up and down. Silver, green or black. When he squeezes me I go *click, clack*. He puts me back down until he turns me upside down. He opens me, smells me. He puts me down and I realise … here we go again!

Mikey Dellinger (12)
Howard of Effingham School

Yes!

Yes! It's the school holidays. Yes! No school for six weeks. Yes! No one to tell me what to do. Yes! I can meet up with friends and have fun. Yes! Holidays. Yes! Beaches and ice cream. Yes! No one's found out I flooded the boys' toilet! No! I'm grounded.

Daniel Bavin

Howard of Effingham School

109

Untitled

I start in a damp dark van. I'm in there for ages,
I finally end up in a soggy place and go into a
factory. I'm packaged and put back into a van. I'm
taken to a shop called WH Smith and put on a
shelf with all my friends.

Eloise Judd
Howard of Effingham School

Anxiety

I can't think of anything worse than getting on
a plane. Your ears pop and you're sitting trying
loads of ways to unpop them and then you find
the one way to unpop them and it hurts like Hell.
Everyone turns round and says, 'Bless you!'

Megan Dann (12)
Howard of Effingham School

Stitches

Blood is pouring out of my hand. My mum is getting our neighbour to take me to the hospital. In the car she puts layers of tea towels over my hand, I bleed through them all. I get to the hospital and have an X-ray. Then I have my stitches.

Michael Wells (11)

Howard of Effingham School

Breathing Underwater

I remember the day when I had my chance to breathe underwater, it was awesome. I was like a fish with gills. My mum bought me a pool to swim in and everything. It came to the next day and that was when I realised that my gills were gone!

Victoria Johnson (11)
Howard of Effingham School

The Beginning

It was cold, his breath so cold. The air froze and shattered at his feet. He could hear memories of lives and voices everywhere. Running, dizziness, confusion everywhere. Soft, light padding reverberating around the black, cold room. He knew that there was a beast. His scream never came out. Silence.

Tom Kempton (13)
Howard of Effingham School

One Day

One day there were lots of chickens in a farm.
They were trying to get out for about three
weeks. They finally got out. They made another
hole to get the horses out. After that they all
went to go and play ball!

Jamie Hastings (11)
Howard of Effingham School

115

The Monster

The shadow reflected on the wall, staring at me.
It scurried over to my bed, footsteps getting
louder. My heart was beating out of my chest. It
jumped. The mouse scurried back into his hole.
The coward.

Hannah Taylor (11)
Howard of Effingham School

The Silent Killer ...

1348 -1350 it struck! Black Death started. People
didn't know what to do, they shut themselves
away, not wanting to catch it. Everything stopped,
the streets were silent!
In 1350 Black Death stopped. People came out of
their houses, the crops could grow. They never
found out what caused it ... !

Heidi Tidman (11)
Howard of Effingham School

117

The Feeling Of Death

It's Year 3. I have the ball. I am running, running, running. The goal - it is in sight, I … I am going to score; *smash!* I'm flying, flying. I'm on the floor, a pool of blood in front of me. The pain. I feel dizzy. I'm going, going, going …

George Davison (11)
Howard of Effingham School

What Colour Shall I Do My Nails?

I am painting my nails pink. Or shall I do them blue? Or shall I do them red? I really don't know. I think and think, then in the end I just do a French manicure. Perfect for me.

Amy Poole (12)
Howard of Effingham School

119

Untitled

Nobody would let me borrow a pencil so I went to the shop and bought a pencil case. I realised that there was nothing to go into it, so I went back to the shop and bought pencils, rubber, sharpener, coloured pencils. Everybody at school loved my stuff.

Megan Lovegrove (11)
Howard of Effingham School

The Robbery

The house is silent. I walk into the spare room
to put my bags away. Files from the cabinets are
scattered all over the floor. I drop my bags and
run out into the hall again. Then I notice the living
room. The window is broken. I scream and
run ...

Vanisha Patel (11)
Howard of Effingham School

Air Hunt

'Ah … the fresh air of a fairy tale, I have never
smelt something so … fresh, like it wasn't real:
a fairy tale.' It was her one, her only, her final
mission. She wanted to make it a gruesome one:
she had to hunt the air. They were on the kill … !

Shanice Pryce (13)
Norbury Manor Business College

Wedding Cries

At 2.30pm Kathy was getting ready for the best day of her life. Her mother was doing her make-up and hair. She put on her lovely, sparkly wedding dress. She got into the car, drove to the church. She walked down the aisle and saw the rings and note.

Kaihanna Hardware (12)

Norbury Manor Business College

123

Wedding Breaker

It was Katie's big day and James looked upset so
as the day went on and the time came for the, 'I
dos', James said, 'I don't … sorry Love I'm in love
with your cousin Paula.'
'Since when?' cried Katie.
'Since the day we met,' replied James.

Rachel Grant (12)
Norbury Manor Business College

My Life's Over

It was Laela's first day at school. 'Wake up!'
shouted her mum, tapping her. She got up and got
ready.
'Bye Mum,' said Laela.
'Bye,' said her mum.
She arrived at school. All the pupils stared at her.
She bumped into a group of bullies. 'Uh oh!'

Abigail Walters (13)
Norbury Manor Business College

Oh Mary!

My heart starts thumping, harder than ever.
I've never been so scared in my whole life. It's
started. It's moving really fast! Round and round.
Moving forward and backwards. Thank God. It's
slowing down now. I get off quick. 'Oh Mary! It's
only a little teacup ride,' Mum says quickly.

Samman Sohail Khan (12)
Norbury Manor Business College

The Dark Alleyway

Monique lay there on the floor of the dark alleyway. *Clip, clop.* She heard footsteps followed by a misty shadow. A male figure appeared. He was coming closer with what looked like a sword. He appeared, 'You OK love?' It was just a high-class man with his pointy umbrella.

Monique Nobrega-Mokogwu (12)
Norbury Manor Business College

Christmas Mystery

She woke up to a rustling sound. Smiling to herself, *It's Santa!* she thought. She swung her legs off the bed. She crept downstairs. Her blue eyes met a hunched shadow. Her brother turned around looking guilty. He had opened all of the Christmas presents.

Henna Shah (12)
Norbury Manor Business College

Flesh

She awoke at the faint sound of tearing flesh. As she walked out of her room, she noticed blood dripping down the stairs. She followed the trail. Emily could now hear the sound louder. She opened the kitchen door to see Ginger hungrily eating the rat, which she was after.

Mahrukh Mirza (12)

Norbury Manor Business College

Midnight Craving

She heard a creak for the third time that night.
She went down to investigate. The creak got
louder as she went down. Her heart thumped
harder with every step she took. She opened the
kitchen door and there was a … 'Sorry Mum, I
got hungry,' I said to her.

Sarah Boubekeur (12)
Norbury Manor Business College

The Figure

It was a chilly autumn day. Emily walked down towards the park. Sitting on the bench, in sight of her, sat a covered figure. It suddenly turned in her direction. 'Emily, is that you?' a familiar voice whispered.

I'd almost forgotten, Grandpa was supposed to meet me here, she thought.

Radiqa Hussain (12)
Norbury Manor Business College

131

Kidnapped

It was noisy and I was surrounded. There was a light shining upon me, everywhere else was dark. I didn't know what to do. Why was I there? The place was drowned by whispers. 'So, what's your name kid?' asked a clown. I was picked to assist a circus act.

Djihane Breteche (12)
Norbury Manor Business College

Into His World ...

He dragged me down. Down into his world.
Through cramped tunnels, dark and dirty. Fear
raged through my body, tore at my heart, my
soul, my mind. Panic surged through my veins.
Still we descended. Where were we going? I saw
light. Faint light. We emerged. There stood evil ...

Bryana Aimable -Lina (13)
Norbury Manor Business College

133

A Squeaking Surprise!

Eek, eek! Karen assumed that someone had broken in. She courageously tiptoed next door, switching on the light, with her hands shaped like a gun. What Karen really heard was the subtle squeaking of mice nibbling on her bread and cheese. Karen screamed and ran out of the room!

Sade Alonge (12)
Norbury Manor Business College

Surprise!

I brushed my shoes on the mat leaving muddy
footsteps behind. I clung onto the stair rail, while
I threw off my shoes. I dragged my tired feet to
the living room. I saw strange figures under the
table. I gasped and headed for the house phone.
'Surprise!' shouted everyone.

Caris Greyson (12)
Norbury Manor Business College

135

The Forest

I was turning and screaming through the pitch-black trees, heart pounding. Then suddenly a light, a bright light was shining at me. I saw a dark figure, holding a lantern. Next I heard a deep voice saying, 'Are you lost? Don't worry I'll help you out of this forest.'

Athena Reid (12)
Norbury Manor Business College

The Footsteps Are Coming

The wind was whistling harshly; thrashing the trees back and forth, the sky was black. Isabelle wrapped her scarf tighter and struggled to keep standing. She could hear footsteps behind her, she stopped dead. Someone tapped her, she turned and started laughing. Her friend held a knife. She stopped laughing.

Toni-Ann Murphy (12)
Norbury Manor Business College

137

Milli And Her Little Brother

Milli went through the park, it was cold. The streetlights were flickering. There was silence. As she walked slowly, she kept hearing rustling noises coming from the bushes. She was terrified …

'Boo!' Milli's little brother shouted. 'Ha, I got you back!' Milli took a deep breath and walked on.

Leterece Carter (13)

Norbury Manor Business College

The Fright

The door slowly creaked open. The bright
light from the hallway flooded my bedroom. A
hunched shadow entered. I froze, petrified. Huge,
bright yellow eyes stared at me. 'Oh, Clem!'
I sighed as I tried to get back to sleep. My cat
jumped onto my bed and purred very loudly.

Nia Samuel Macey (12)
Norbury Manor Business College

The Unknown

Emma walked through the dark woods alone.
The trees' bony hands were reaching out for
her. A twig snapped, so she began to run. Seeing
a dark figure move through the woods, Emma
looked down and ran faster. Suddenly she
bumped into something.
'Emma, are you okay?' her mother asked.

Nishita Patel (12)
Norbury Manor Business College

Panic

He paced up and down wondering where the
bride was. He was getting impatient. He was
panicking, people started to go. She was over 3
hours late. It was obvious she wasn't coming. The
groom was having a bad day. It got worse when
… *plop!* Bird poo all over him.

Chante Wright (12)
Norbury Manor Business College

Killed And Killed Again

As she sat up in her grave, her skin was death white. She looked around quickly, she suddenly saw the girl who she almost killed. Then with a shock of light she felt pain. She'd been shot that moment in time. She was killed and killed again.

Flavia Small (12)

Norbury Manor Business College

A Dream Is A Wish

She was lying on the bed holding a picture of Juliet
to her heart. 'I wish I could be her,' she sighed.
The doorbell rang. She opened the door.
'Hello love,' he said. She fell on the floor.
'It came true,' she said, holding her hands on her
heart.

Nisha Gor (12)
Norbury Manor Business College

143

Magic Carpet

'There's the lamp!'
'Hurry Bimbo, grab on!'
Whoosh! The carpet flew in the air and Aladdin
grabbed the lamp and the carpet flew straight out
just in time. Aladdin rubbed the lamp and a genie
appeared.
'I can grant you any wish,' said the genie. Aladdin
and Bimbo smiled …

Zainab Rahim (12)
Norbury Manor Business College

Surprise

'I bet everyone's forgotten my birthday,' I
groaned.
'Oh, stop moaning. They didn't forget,' Mum said,
annoyed.
'Yes they did.'
'Give me those bags and get the rest,' Mum said.
'Oh Ok,' I said. I walked into the house and
- 'Surprise! You thought we'd forgotten your
birthday!'

Aida Hassan (12)
Norbury Manor Business College

UFO

'Nobody is here. Wait, Komal is walking to school. Press the button. We nearly have everyone. You missed her!'

'Shut up!'

'Wait, she's seen us. She's running. Press the button! Yesss!'

'Argh!' said Komal.

'Right we have got her. Got everyone now.'

'Right, fly back to home. Mother is waiting.'

Georgia Jones (13)

Norbury Manor Business College

Thunderbolt - Yes!

The theme park was packed with candy kids. Rossete and Andrew were best friends. They approached Thunderbolt. Rossete wanted to take her new camera on Thunderbolt but it clearly said: *No Loose Items*. Whilst taking pictures the camera fell, the strap got tangled. *Boom!* The ride exploded. Thunderbolt was gone!

Anieshka Mido

Norbury Manor Business College

147

Knock, Knock, Knock

Gasping for breath Georgia rushed to the head
teacher's office. *Knock, knock, knock.*
'Come in,' he said.
'Sir, you called.'
'Yes Georgia, actually I wanted … '
Knock, knock, knock.
'I'll get it.'
'Is Mr Sands there?'
'Yes, come in.'
'Mr Sands, Bethany's here for you. Mr Sands,
where did you go?'

Komal Kamran (12)
Norbury Manor Business College

148

Shattered World

Tears she cried as she combed her lean, almost grey hair with her long bony fingers. She looked through the shattered pieces of glass, hoping to find some beauty in her ghostly face. But there was no more beauty nor laughter in her life. She was all alone.

Lucy Greer (13)
Norbury Manor Business College

149

Suffering Thunder!

A crack! A boom! Preparing for a quick attack!
Gloomy clouds are taking charge and drops of
rain trickle down your numb skin. A cold breeze
rushes against your face and everything seems
different: alone, cold and the moment's intense.
Why did you leave your umbrella at home?

Zara Rathod (12)
Norbury Manor Business College

Waiting To Be Found

Lying there waiting to be found, watching people pass. My hair is knotted. My coat is wet, desperate to be wanted. I can't believe they left me, really thought they loved me. No water, so cold, so hungry. Really thought they wanted me … Only to be found by the RSPCA.

Antoinette Smith (12)

Norbury Manor Business College

Shivers!

The surface is as white as polar bears' fur. I feel the breeze slash across my face. I'm cold, can't feel my toes. I need help! No one will save me from this cold, damp world. Am I all alone? I have three words for you … I hate ice-skating!

Karise Yansen (12)

Norbury Manor Business College

Amongst The Clouds

I was drifting away on a bubble amongst the weightless, fluffy clouds, when all of a sudden I was falling down through the sky, skipping and turning, plummeting to my death. I pinched myself … only a dream. Must be. I snapped my eyes open. Was I in Heaven or Hell?

Keziah Tay (12)
Norbury Manor Business College

153

The Wardrobe

Lucy stared into the wardrobe. There was a noise, a quiet bang. She cuddled Mr Bunny and went inside her duvet. Lucy's heartbeat went faster and faster every second, as the noise grew louder and louder. There was silence … The door creaked open. Then Lucy heard, 'Were you scared, Sis?'

Sujanie Kaneshamoorthy (12)
Norbury Manor Business College

Burning

It looked unbearable, the flames gathering,
the heat looked intense. The cadmium red
and glittering yellow, together forever. People
screaming, babies crying. A child lying on its back,
knocked out by the fumes. The smoke covering
the city like a smoky blanket, pouncing like a lion.
My painting finally finished.

Sabrina Ilori (13)
Norbury Manor Business College

155

Elegant Green

As the spectators take their seats, a family lie still.
They have pale skin and matching hair. They wear
elegant green dresses over their slim bodies.
They are identical to each other. Then, they are
separated and one by one, those same lilies are
thrown on to the grave.

Holly-Louise Howlett (12)
Norbury Manor Business College

The Sneeze From Afar

One day in the park, Jemma and I were on
the crimson swings. The birds were chirping.
Suddenly a sneeze came from afar and the whole
world changed. The swings we were on changed
into flash cars, which we happened to be driving!
My amazing yet petrifying dream, rapidly over!

Roberta Wedderburn (12)

Norbury Manor Business College

157

The Unknown Footprint

Yesterday on my way to school, I saw something, something so abnormal, so extraordinary, so beyond this world. It was a footprint! But no ordinary footprint, its texture and features were beyond imagination! But what could it have been? Who knew? All I knew was it was an unknown footprint.

Okpejevwe Ejoh (12)
Norbury Manor Business College

Silence

The door was slightly ajar when Bryana returned
home. She called into the gloom, no one
answered. Bryana crept upstairs as she could hear
a noise up there. She slammed the door quickly.
As it opened, someone screamed. It was only
Nia, she had forgotten to close the door!

Tamara Achampong (12)
Norbury Manor Business College

159

Late Night

It was late at night and I couldn't sleep. I was huddled in my bed. Suddenly I heard footsteps downstairs. I was terrified. I got out of my bed and tiptoed downstairs. I peeped round the corner and it turned out to be my mum drinking a mug of tea!

Yashita Patel (12)
Norbury Manor Business College

The Dark Night

It was dark, pitch-black, everywhere was silent. She walked through the door but her parents were nowhere to be seen. Suddenly something jumped on her head. 'Fluffy get off me.' It was the stupid cat. *Phew,* she thought, *I'm safe.* But was she? Someone tapped her shoulder, she screamed.

Sana Rehman (13)
Norbury Manor Business College

Look Mum!

She slowly opened the door, carefully peeping inside. She saw some powder footprints and heard loud splashes. She came closer and saw that the water was splattered everywhere. She picked up the courage and stepped forward. 'Mum!' she shouted, 'no! I don't want to take a bath, Mum. Muuuum!'

Mahnoor Mirza (12)

Norbury Manor Business College

Shuffling Behind The Bag

Ding-dong. There at the door was Aunt Mary, who
was smiling. She told me to make myself at home
and to put my bags in the spare room. I heard
something croaking, something was shuffling
behind the bag. I turned around slowly to find a
puppy chewing the cushion!

Ryanne Baptiste-Young (12)
Norbury Manor Business College

163

Silence

It was getting very late. Mum was expecting me back by nine. The quickest way home was through the deserted park. I heard a rustle and hustle. Loud steps came closer and closer. Silence. As I turned … 'Oh I'm sorry, I thought you stole the sweets from my sweet shop.'

Kinari Shah (13)
Norbury Manor Business College

The Cook

He sprinkled in the herbs and handed over the spoon, he started shaking. What would it be like? Would they think it was disgusting or would they think it was delicious and boost him up to stardom? It was one fixed point in time but could change his life forever.

Georgia Edginton-Vigus (13)
Rosebery School

Life Or Death

Bang! went the gun. He looked behind and started to run. There was fear dripping from his nose. Thump, thump went his heartbeat. The rushing of his breath. His legs begged him stop but his head said no. Pushing, pushing come on. 'Lucas Smith has won the 200m race!'

Emmanuelle Godinho (12)
Rosebery School

Eternal Darkness

The man screamed, writhing in pain on the
floor. The sky was a blanket of darkness and the
moon full, the only source of light in the sparkling
sky. The ground was sodden with blood, and a
vaporous mist surrounded his body. Death was
rapidly closing in. He knew it.

Polly Marquis (13)
Rosebery School

Lightning

The grey sky loomed overhead. The rain beat down in torrents from the scudding swirl of mist, fog and clouds. She reached for the doorknob and twisted it. A chink of lightning cracked like a whip and she fell to the ground.
Don't ever go out in a storm.

Emma Charlotte Thomas (12)
Rosebery School

Chains

Her eyes glistened with tears as she looked
down at the chains binding her hands. Just a bit
of metal but it deprived her of her freedom.
Everything she owned, now nothing. It meant
nothing to anyone. She was nothing. The chains
pulled on her hands, beckoning her to follow …

Charlotte Whellams (14)
Rosebery School

169

This Was It

It was all there, the proof, the proof that she had done it. The proof that she had murdered him and that was all they needed, all they needed to lock her away forever. She could feel her breath being taken away, her guts twisting her insides. This was it.

Isabelle Coombes (12)

Rosebery School

Dragon's Dawn

High up amongst the mountains a dragon opens his eyes, flexing and yawning. Looking out in the air, his brothers are waiting. He makes his run and leaps to the sky, wings expanded and ready to soar. They fly off into the climbing sun. It's time to go to war.

Martin Norman (17)

Strodes College

The Mummy

It was dark; silent. The smell musty; old. The air full of dust. A bang; a moan. The mummy. He moved, edging out of the darkness, creeping, moaning. He was going to kill us, I was sure. He was closer. Running into the light, we locked him in the tomb.

Kayleigh-Rae Philp-Wernham (17)

Strodes College

The Goblin's Gold

The goblin lay in gold.
'Its mine! Ha!' The door swung open.
'Evil creature!' The man pulled out his sword.
Clang!
They fought until, 'Argh!' They sunk into the gold,
like quicksand. The man grabbed the statue, but
the goblin vanished.
'All hail the man who gave to the poor!'

Karishma Puri (16)
Strodes College

173

Untitled

Speed was essential. He looked back once and instantly regretted it. Now speed was vital for his survival. It was literally unheard of. Full combat helicopters bearing down on unarmed villages occupied by women and young children. The rotors beat a soft rhythm. The pilot turned away gently. He fired.

Mohamed Saed (16)

Strodes College

Pictures Of Heroes

Starstruck young hearts rushed across the endless moor. A few metres away the glinting film caravan encompassed our youth and passion. Like on TV, floppy hair, northern accents. They peered at our muddied clothes. Anguish paid off! *Snap! Click!* they posed playfully. Signed Paul, George, John, Ringo. Dreams accomplished!

Alivia Castle (16)

Strodes College

Firestarter

He was the trouble starter. For he was smarter than those fear-addicted. The dragon was the firestarter. He ran faster than the dragon could master. For the fire blaster was the flaming instigator. He ran further from the firestarter. He overcame the fire master. He lived happily ever after.

Thomas Bassett (17)

Strodes College

Parking Space

Finally we find a space! We speed full pelt towards it, stealing it from all the other cars. We climb out of the car into the chilly Christmas Eve air. We then pile on all our coats, gloves, hats and scarves then brave our descent to the theatre.

Charley Herdman (16)

Strodes College

177

The Long-Awaited Treat

The brandy caught fire and flared up, making the shape hard to distinguish in the dark. Salivating with excitement, I sank my spoon like a knife in the heart of my dark and rich victim. Total explosion! The taste shattered the roof of my mouth! Another Christmas, another great pudding!

Anemone Jasmin-Baker (17)

Strodes College

Untitled

Flashing eyes and bitter words. Last night is all a haze. Wake me up before you go, let's clear the stormy air. I press against you, we embrace and you kiss me with open eyes. The night is done, our own strange world, and I love you to the day.

Tess Wright (16)
Strodes College

179

Untitled

I woke up, rolled over … I landed on his pillow,
the smell, his smell … almost vanilla-like with
a hint of fresh berries was … gone. His keys
always carelessly left on the side table … gone …
I retraced the last steps he took, just to breathe
some life into this life.

Tanya Chahal (17)
Strodes College

The Dandelion

An old woman cradled a dandelion in her
weathered palms, guiding the seedlings into the
safety of the grass with her breath, to thrive in
the sunlight, leaving the deseeded plant on the
ground.
That evening, drunken strangers crushed the
dandelion underfoot. Like the strangers, it would
no longer thrive.

Lucy-Ann Brandon (17)
Strodes College

181

Saturday Night In Albion

Darkness fell over Albion. Markus stepped onto the cobbled pathway. He walked, footsteps making barely any sound. Arriving at Lillian's home, he peered into the darkness. Her delicate features appeared before him. Her scent perfumed the air around him. Her soft fingers linked between his. They walked, bathed in starlight.

Jack Xabier Lugg (17)
Strodes College

Onwards

The old man, decrepit and frail with age,
had seen it all - everything. The universe had
exhausted all it could offer. Yet with death came
something new; a different challenge, a final gift.
He was pleased with this challenge, up for it.
Death did not need provoking. It came quietly.

Joseph Jones (17)
Strodes College

Cold Prison

I woke up in cold and dark nothingness. I
couldn't see or move. I smelt rotting flesh.
Footsteps filled my ears and crept up my spine.
With sudden force and tumult, one of the walls
shifted beside me. I tumbled haphazardly out of
the fridge and into my back garden.

Kirsty Edwards-Capes (16)
Strodes College

Mince Pies

The mince pies, resplendent in red and green
packaging, beamed proudly from their rows
at the buzzing Christmas shoppers. Aglow
with festivity, they nudged forward with silent
anticipation, trying to beat their fellows into the
festive shopping basket.
I like mince pies - why give them glory only once
a year?

Hazel Edwards (17)
Strodes College

185

Christmas Surprise

Mum gives Ben Robot Junior for Christmas. At night Robot Junior trashes the room.
In the morning he escapes out of the window and leaves behind a bomb timed to explode in ten minutes. Robot Junior finds his spacecraft and flies back to Custard Planet. The whole world blows up!

Sean Crayden
The Link Secondary School

Jesus And Richard

A generation of gangsters carrying guns, gleaming gun metal, grotesque grave fillers. Richard lay down, pondering the question. *Surely Jesus will stop the bad guys,* he thought, he believed in God. The door crashed open. Richard faced a shotgun. The gun exploded backwards, guilty intruder, extinct. Did Jesus save Richard?

Jake Sutherland (14)

The Link Secondary School

Twins

Twins known as Mini and Airi absolutely hate each other. They always argue. Their best friend Yuna thinks they get along because she stops the arguments. But then it is discovered that her friend is missing. Can they stop fighting or will they split up?

Jessica Lannon (14)
The Link Secondary School

The Diver Who Never Said His Name

The secret diver kicked his flippers, breathed in the air from his tank and dived under the waves. He swam through seaweed, fish and carefully through sharks to explore the shipwreck. He suddenly saw a ghost then he quickly swam back, but he was lost in the sea. Ghost's revenge?

Iain King (15)

The Link Secondary School

The Chase

The rabbit scampered across the moist ground.
The hungry fox was desperate for food. The
hopeless, insignificant rabbit had no chance. It
rapidly ran, but the fox was always directly behind
him. A rabbit burrow caught the rabbit's eye.
It scurried inside. The fox miserably wandered
home without a meal.

Annabel Moore (12)
Tormead School

Footprints That Never End

Iola pulled her coat around her as she walked through the desert, it was a cold night. She was following the footprints. They went on and on, seeming never to end. The sand lingered in her toes as she continued forwards and followed the footprints that never ended.

Charlotte Geary (12)
Tormead School

191

The Killing

I clutched the knife, bloodstained from the first cut. Its unnerving eyes stared lifelessly at me. Its slimy tentacles limp at its side. Midnight ink leaked out of it. I couldn't do it, I couldn't! I picked up the octopus' body and threw it in the trash.

Sarah Wills (13)
Tormead School

The Lucky Light

Sally walked through the garden. She had
nowhere to go as the padlock was on the church
door. It was raining and her new shirt was black
with dirt. When she was about to give up hope
some Ford lights appeared and she was taken
home to her welcoming house.

Nicola Hoy (13)
Tormead School

193

Trail Of Footsteps

I touched the footprint with my fingertips, feeling the muddy ridge around the edge and the smooth sole. The trail of footprints disappeared around the corner, so crouching carefully down I peered round. A shape loomed down on me and I shut my eyes tightly as ...the dog licked me!

Josephine Darwin (12)

Tormead School

Mum Lost It Again

'Mum, it's not fair! Why can't I go shopping?
I'll do my homework later,' said Millie as her
mother got impatient. They had been having this
conversation for fifteen minutes and it wasn't
getting anywhere. Finally Millie's mum lost it and
yelled, 'Go! As long as you be quiet!'

Alice Taylor-Peat (12)
Tormead School

The Darkness

I turned and ran. The footsteps closer, louder, less careful. I knew it was coming, the darkness seeping through my vision like a dream. Suddenly a shot pierced the air. The darkness disappeared. Mary strode confidently from behind me, gun in hand. Her lopsided grin was mirrored on my face.

Emily Samuels (12)
Tormead School

Cheating

Stuck! Algebra! The test paper stared up at me like an ugly goblin! I blamed the teacher, he never told our class about 2x and 30x. I had two options; I could use my talented mind to figure out the answer or cheat! I chose to cheat and I did.

Rebecca Smith (12)
Tormead School

197

The Falling Christmas Tree

As Johnny and Lisa finished putting the
decorations on the Christmas tree, the door
opened and their father came in. The dog, in the
excitement of it all, pelted towards the tree. It
came down with a crash. Father groaned and
went upstairs to fetch the two-foot, synthetic
tree.

Megan Wishart (12)

Tormead School

An Oxymoron

Thunder crashed tearing leaves down. Lightning
lit up the sky in flashes of white light. Behind a
bush that quaked in the vicious wind a feeble
neigh wasn't heard. The newly born foal's first
glance was Mother Nature's obvious wrath.
On a night of mass destruction, new life is found.

Saskia Mathias (12)
Tormead School

199

The Opening

'Open it!' whispered Kirsty. A dark rotting chest sat in front of the two scared twins.

'No! We should not be here,' replied Jake. He heaved the chest back into the dark dismal cupboard. 'It started that way and therefore it's going to finish that way.'

'Fine,' Kirsty mumbled angrily.

Melissa Williams (12)

Tormead School

Read The Sign!

I woke up from my bed, gazing at my alarm
clock. The time was 8 o'clock. I was late! I
stumbled out into the streets of China! I started
scrambling through mothers and children.
Finally, I'd arrived. Then I managed to catch sight
of a sign saying: 'Closed on Saturdays.'

Aneesa Zaman (12)
Tormead School

201

Deep Sleep

I woke in a magical land with flowers covered in
a thick fluffy layer of snow. My bare feet making
footprints as I walked. Suddenly there was a
bang! It all disappeared! Something was walking
towards me. It was dark and humid …
'Darling wake up, it's nearly time for school.'

Alex Adams (12)

Tormead School

The Mystery

The footprints remained in the sand for just a moment then disappeared under the water. All sorts of things landed on the island each year. But this was nothing like the things anyone had seen before. No one dared to approach it. It is still there today, slowly breathing.

Phoebe Nicklin (12)
Tormead School

The Race

Lily pushed hard on her back foot, rocking forward. She was neck and neck with a St Catherine's girl. The girl was fast but Lily had trained and passed her easily. She sped on along the final stretch. With one last burst of energy she threw herself over the line.

Alice Booth (12)
Tormead School

The Beach

Crash! Azure sea slammed upon sandy shore. A young girl darted towards it, her eyes glistening and bubbling, full of excitement! She had persuaded her mum but she was reluctant at first. She blinked her eyes and … *splash!* A bottlenose swam with her on its back!

Taniesha Kadiri (11)
Wallington High School For Girls

Blood And Flesh

Peeping around the kitchen door, I saw a knife and red stuff; blood. Then I saw pale stuff; flesh. I heard laughter and the shadow grew nearer. I ran behind the couch. The shadow came even closer and I screamed. Then my brother presented me with a jam sandwich.

Maya Bolaky (11)
Wallington High School For Girls

The Other Side Of Santa

'Santa Claus is just a cover. *Grrr,* this child wants a TV! We're gonna 'ave to fix me old one. I think it's about time I got a new one! Kids these days actually expect me to get them new things. Time to get the cheesy act on … Merry Christmas!'

Arjuna Shandramohan (12)

Wallington High School For Girls

Emotions

Tears streaming down her face, the door
slammed shut. Her heart felt as if it was going
to rip out of her chest. She ran to her desk and
scribbled down a note. She peered out of her
bedroom window. She could never trust anyone
ever again!

Zubia Khan (12)

Wallington High School For Girls

Ocean Of Terror

I gazed into the dark blue depths of the water.
I stood petrified, certain I could see murky
figures lurking at the bottom. I imagined sharks
swimming, waiting to get me as I made the first
cold plunge.
'Argh!' I shrieked as my sister shoved me into the
swimming pool.

Nicole Jashapara (12)
Wallington High School For Girls

209

Sunday Lunch

The farmer grabbed any lamb near to him. We all knew what was going to happen. We'd get turned into Sunday lunch.

'Baah!' I blurted.

'Put down your gun, you're under arrest!' bellowed a distant voice.

'W-w-why?' stuttered the farmer.

'You're gonna be my dinner!' Mrs Farmer assured him.

Winnie Healy (11)

Wallington High School For Girls

The Christmas Treat!

Everyone sat around the glorious Christmas tree, waiting to open their wrapped presents. They counted seconds until midnight.

'5, 4, 3, 2, 1, Merry Christmas,' shouted everyone, opening their presents. Taking a deep breath, Lucy opened her present and *pop* out came a clown. It had scared her life out!

Soumya Jud (11)
Wallington High School For Girls

The Skull Of Santa Claus

The sacred skull was in the deserted house in its pride of place. The girl cautiously removed it, unwisely. The girl ran out of the house and in her rush dropped the skull into the nearby pond. The house burst into flames, leaving her beloved brother behind.

Sinead Bouattaf (11)
Wallington High School For Girls

Beast

The beast was rising from the shadows, its hungry
eyes glistening in the moonlight. Its head was
dripping with blood! I screamed, I was rooted
to the spot, frozen with terror. It snarled at me,
leapt forward, then it all went dark. The lights
flooded back. I left the cinema.

Nashmeeya Ayyaz (12)
Wallington High School For Girls

Evil Teddy

I went into my bed and hugged my teddy. When I
looked at him, his black eyes turned green and he
spoke, 'I'll kill you!' His claws came alive and he
scratched my face and blood was dripping and my
flesh came out. Bye bye …
'And cut! Great scene everyone!'

Amrita Gill (11)
Wallington High School For Girls

Red-Eyed Devil

Zap! The red-eyed girl killed the baby so innocent, so delicate. My gran warned me about her type, I thought she was joking. I saw a poster of the girl in the shop, I was disgusted. Then, out of the blue, her eyes stared across the room …

Kalema Powell (11)
Wallington High School For Girls

215

Knock, Knock!

The exquisite tree was up and decorated with golden and red tinsel and presents wrapped up in paper! I heard a raucous knock at the door. It was Santa Claus. He gave us some presents, ate our mince pie and drink milk. We sat down to a delicious dinner!

Amatullah Adamjee (11)
Wallington High School For Girls

Painting

Stares, trapped, permanent but living. Their
smiles so cold although their eyes are so alive,
that is the woe of a painting. The gallery is hugged
in darkness. *Flash*, but just for a second. Her eyes
flicker for the first time in 500 years. Van Gogh's
monster is now released!

Vickie Bowran (12)
Wallington High School For Girls

My Hero

As I entered the room, I could hear sniggering.
Anywhere I approached people moved away
from me.
At lunchtime, I was the only one without pudding.
In the playground, the class played catch with my
blazer. Then popular Lucy came over.
'Leave her alone!' she screamed. Lucy was my
hero!

Sajna Haneefa (11)
Wallington High School For Girls

Bedtime Journey

Through forests of green, around mountains of grey, on seas of blue … where do I go? No one knows but me. The part of the day I look forward to most …ready to lose myself in my bedtime journey in my dreams!

Bethany Knowles (12)
Wallington High School For Girls

219

The Ticket

She carefully stepped out of the car. Her mum nudged her forward. She grasped the ticket and gave it to the man, 'Thank you for purchasing a ticket for Toy Story 3D!'
She was so angry, she had to go and see Toy Story with her little brother. How unfair!

Lara Kneeshaw (11)

Wallington High School For Girls

Spooked

Cold sweat trickled down his face. He ran.
Footsteps pounded down the alleyway.
'No, no, no!' he screamed in terror. 'Stop, help,
don't hurt me.'
'Are you watching horror movies again?' asked
his mum. 'I told you not to, you'll get nightmares.
Turn off the TV now!'

Philippa Caunter (11)
Wallington High School For Girls

221

Drowning

Splash! I descended into the clear blue water.
Bubbles moved all around me. I was moving
slowly, drifting through the water. My eyes started
to sting as I looked around the surrounding area.
Nothing was clear to me.
'John, let's get some training done in this
swimming lesson! Ha! Ha!'

Imogen Bristow (11)
Wallington High School For Girls

Creeped

Creak! I spun round. Nothing. I began to feel my skin crawl. I listened. There it was again. I made the same swift move as I did before and all that was to be seen was a ghastly creature creeping rapidly into the shadowy depths of intense death.

Ellie Hammett (11)

Wallington High School For Girls

223

The Voice

What is it? Standing there, staring right at me?
Turning, glaring, there is no escape in sight! What
could that be?
'Come hither child,' it speaks sharply. I recognise
the voice. The shadow hides its identity. As it
walks towards me, into the light, I recognise Dad,
laughing at me!

Chloe Bishop-Wright (11)
Wallington High School For Girls

Hungry Predator

I pounced on it like a predator clawing at its skin
and hacking ravenously at the insides. It spattered
all over the floor in a heap of mush and I glared
at it with dark glittering eyes, giving a great howl.
Mum frowned, but tossed me a new banana.

Rachel Barham (11)
Wallington High School For Girls

Running

Venus looked over her shoulder and stared into the man's piercing eyes. Then Venus looked back to the path she was running on and realised she was about to go over the edge. She quickly jumped out of the way and carelessly the man went straight over the cliff edge.

Emily O'Dell (11)
Wallington High School For Girls

Burnt

I sat there as the heat coursed through my body; it burned like a fire in my mouth. My eyes began to water and I turned crimson. I gulped down some water. Relief! I hate jalapenos.

Mairisa Spiers (12)

Wallington High School For Girls

Morning Adventure

I crept, stealthily, dodging and ducking, starting and stopping, peeping and pattering. Her eyes open at the sound of my small movements. She glared around the room. Did she notice me? Her eyes then gradually closed. *Phew!* I crept into the room. 'Wake up, I want breakfast!'

Jessica Read (12)
Wallington High School For Girls

Strips ...

The young cub ran for its life for the hungry tiger had set its bulbous eyes upon him! It raged and slashed at the innocent cub! Suddenly, a howling scream was cacophonous; the tiger galloped away leaving the relieved cub at its mother's side.

Georgeena Reid Lloyd (11)
Wallington High School For Girls

The Monster!

It's ugly, it's green, the thing's coming closer to me. What with the stinky breath, I can't bear it anymore. I run to the corner of my room, then it says, 'Do you wanna play footie?' Oh it's only my brother!

Samantha Beeton (12)
Wallington High School For Girls

Ghostly Nightmare

The wooden door slowly groaned open as I entered the haunted house, mice everywhere, darting, scuttling, from one corner to the next. I peered up the winding staircase and a pale white figure came floating towards me. The next thing I knew I was floating amongst them.

Rachel Dyson (11)
Wallington High School For Girls

231

Pages Of Horror

The wolf jumped, teeth sank into soft flesh. I gasped out loud! The girl fell to the floor shrieking in pain! I willed for her to get up, but my hopes fell as quickly as they rose. She lay on the floor dead ...
I turned the page, what a book!

Maddy O'Neil (12)
Wallington High School For Girls

Werewolf

I was tiptoeing and froze until I saw a ravenous
starving werewolf. I turned pale. Brown, with
demonising red blood and bloodshot eyes, the fur
acted like sharp spikes and its claws were ready
to pounce and kill. I screamed in fear!
It … it was my brother on Hallowe'en!

Samiha Hussain (11)
Wallington High School For Girls

Unusual Meeting

Endless thoughts about the meat, so succulent, juicy. I could almost smell the delicious beauty; it shone in front of me engulfed in a bun and thick scarlet sauce. My teeth sank into the juicy beef of their own accord, my wife with piercing eyes yelled, 'Darling, you're a vegetarian!'

Simran Bains (12)

Wallington High School For Girls

Black Or White

The king shuffled to his left as an act of defence,
but immediately regretted his choice. The man
on horseback, who had been biding his time
opposite, galloped forwards and then turned to
block the king's only exit. As the king bowed
his head in defeat, the knight shouted …
'Checkmate!'

Alina Merchant-Mohamed (12)
Wallington High School For Girls

Raging Porcelain Hole

She was whirled, hurtled, crashed onto sharp jagged teeth. The whirlwind of aqua corkscrewed itself until she was engulfed into the mists of the cavern. My Barbie had been drowned in the toilet.

Simran Sehdev (11)

Wallington High School For Girls

Lily's Big Moment

Lily was practising very hard for her big day - the
annual school awards evening. Lily was going to
perform! Whilst she was practising she fell! Lily
worried all night, what if this happened on the big
day tomorrow?
The next day, Lily's mum said to her, 'Just believe
in yourself!'

Pooja Sunildath (12)
Wallington High School For Girls

237

Accidents Happen

All I could see was water. The cool clear liquid rushing around me – sometimes in small trickles but also gushing like the Niagara Falls. I bobbed along on top the frothing waves, water flooding all around me …

I howled with embarrassment and hauled my wet sheets to the bathroom. Again.

Thanika Thillaivasan (11)

Wallington High School For Girls

The Shadow

I stood stationary, staring into the doorway. It was a murderer, just a shadow of one, holding a knife, plodding towards me whispering my name. When it was at breathing distance from me I flicked the light on …
'Oh 'ello love, y'wanna biscuit?' Granny made great cookies.

Katherine Corcoran (11)
Wallington High School For Girls

Panic!

Bang! A gunshot. Glancing down, I saw blood then everything went black. I couldn't see, I couldn't hear, I couldn't speak. What happened? I woke up shrieking. After all that, it was only a dream, a nightmare. Why me? The panic was over.

Jess Randall (11)
Wallington High School For Girls

Perfect Place

Lily stumbled out of the car, clutching her teddy
bear, when she heard the jazzy music. Staring in
awe she dropped her beautiful brown bear, as it
was so wonderful.

'Lily dear,' her mother said sweetly. 'This is only
the entrance, let's go in!'

Lindsay Farquhar (11)
Wallington High School For Girls

Enemies

Searching the gloomy alleys, watching though there is nothing to see. Shuffling a distance away a boy comes out with a pistol pointed to me. I raise mine. He cackles … I scream. *Bang!* He's shot me. I feel the drops of wetness trickle over me … I really hate water fights!

Jessica Hay (12)
Wallington High School For Girls

Home Sweet Home

Our new house, brilliant for the family. It's new
and quite expensive. We all walk in … it is really
horrid and sticky. Then we remember, *oh yeah,
it's a house made of sweets. Liquorice wands,
gingerbread, Smarties. A wonderful sweet little home
for us all!*

Abby St John (11)
Wallington High School For Girls

The Wrong World

Ella stared at her face in the mirror. Her eyes were gleaming green with beauty as her light blonde hair blew across her face. Suddenly, her face turned and twisted out of shape and so did the rest of her surroundings!
'Are the clothes ready yet Ella?'

Joyce Chan (11)
Wallington High School For Girls

Christmas

It is white and cold - it's Christmas! Children are warm and some children are cold but they have fun in the snow. I am playing in the snow and then someone throws a snowball at my friend. I throw one back then it is even.

Ricky Allen (11)
West Hill School

The Fastest Hedgehog Alive

Look over there! It has spikes. It's blue; it wears red and white shoes. It's faster than the speed of sound. It's a race car … No! It's a jet plane … No! It's a rocket … No! It's Sonic the Hedgehog! The world's fastest hedgehog!

Artendy Malik (12)
West Hill School

The Simpsons Versus Austin Powers

The Simpsons and Austin Powers had a fight after Homer said to Austin, 'You are a weakling,' Austin decided that they would have a match: Minime vs Bart. Minime popped Bart's eyes out with a mini champagne bottle. Minime left Bart bleeding to death in the soggy bubbles.

Ciaran Marren (11)

West Hill School

The Horse Race

It's race day. My horse is called Buttons. We are
at the starting gates at Ascot Race Course. We are
off, zooming into the lead. We jump all the fences
and win the race! We are crowned champions of
the world 2009 and are given a trophy.
'Well done Buttons!'

Cory Andrews (11)
West Hill School

The Monster

The monster was staring, taunting me with its big eyes. I stared back because I was too scared to run. My heart was pounding over not knowing its next move. So I threw some bombs. *Boom!* The monster ran away.

I shouted, 'Yes! End of the level. Finally!'

Thomas Judge (15)
West Hill School

Dream Of A Lifetime

It's finally come! The dream of being on stage is here! No turning back, I can feel it! The adrenalin pumping through veins, the crowd cheering, me under the spotlight, the fame! This is it, my special moment, my time to … *dring!*
'Henry, time to get up for school!'

Gareth Sims-Brassett (15)
West Hill School

Mina Freeman

Once upon a time there was a girl called Mina,
the most optimistic girl in the world. Her mum
and dad were explorers, travelling the North Pole
to the South Pole. Mina didn't know why but she
wished she'd never gone exploring. Maybe she
fell off a cliff?

Amy Jo Armstrong (11)
West Hill School

251

Mini Mad Race

Between Maddy, Bobby and Glutty. Maddy shot
ahead. Bobby crashed on the next corner. Glutty
stalled but what was this? Bobby was back! Maddy
finished first, Glutty came second and Bobby
didn't finish the race. He broke down on the
twentieth corner. Too bad for Bobby!

Alex Gostling (11)
West Hill School

Spirit

Once upon a time there was a girl called Amy.
She was invited to a party. Amy saw this boy at
the party. The boy asked Amy for a dance. Amy
thought he was really nice. He was a ghost; Amy
was in for a shock!

Hannah Smyth (12)
West Hill School

253

Ghost Motorbike

Frank's mum bought him a motorbike for his birthday. Frank's mum made him promise not to go fast. Frank promised he wouldn't go fast. Frank did not keep this promise.

One night the police came to the door …

At night Frank's mum still hears his motorbike going down the lane …

Simon Brown (13)

West Hill School

Paradox

'Entering Japan,' said the radio. The pilot in the
plane couldn't believe what he was doing.
'Above Hiroshima, countdown, 5, 4, 3, 2, 1,' said
the radio. He couldn't do it. His plane flew off.
The shadow man grinned. A rift opened.
'It begins,' rasped the shadow man.

Muntej Chana (13)
Wilson's School

Untitled

The burglar walked slowly to the new car and *bam!* He broke the window, got in and drove away. The police were on his tail. *Bang, bang, bang!* The tyres were shot. He shielded off the road, he was wounded badly and was put in jail for stealing a car.

Duncan Antony (13)
Wilson's School

The Man Who Smiled

The man plunged into the ocean and the sharks feasted. The woman's head erupted in a red pulp. The explosion lit up the city, the diplomats were vaporised. The plane plummeted and the passengers' screams were silenced. And as the deaths took place simultaneously the man smiled. It had begun.

Philip Knott (12)
Wilson's School

257

Trapped

His evil master forced him in, the door slammed shut behind him. Trapped! Jack knew it would end this way but he never expected it to happen so soon. In front of him was a melting zebra with a moustache.

Jack loathed art school trips. Why was art so unusual?

George Barbantan (12)

Wilson's School

Bang!

How did I get myself into this mess? thought
Kieran, tied to a chair above sticks of dynamite.
The fuses were short and Kieran knew his death
was near. Two seconds passed then … *bang!*
Kieran's head dropped on the floor. Blood was
everywhere. Body bits were sprawled around the
room.

Shaun Carpenter (12)
Wilson's School

Terror Attack

Rounds of gunfire crackled Jack's ears. His family now dead, his town blown to pieces. He saw many masked men shooting at pedestrians. Jack was glued to the spot. Suddenly, his heart was thumping. They saw him! He bolted for cover. Jack was being chased down, his heart stopped beating …

Tahmid Rashid (12)

Wilson's School

Untitled

Oliver jumped. Seconds later the bomb exploded
below him. As he landed, a spray of shots flew
past. Oliver ducked down, hoping to ambush the
enemy. He leaped up, finding only a jet of water
hitting him. Dripping, he glared up at his friend
who was smiling at another victory.

Elliott Kasoar (12)
Wilson's School

Somewhere Out There

' Abort! Abort! Aliens have captured Jack in a base of theirs!' The army had to do something. Pay-out was what sprung to mind. They offered them £20,000, they refused. The army went in and killed the aliens. Jack was safe but he knew there were more somewhere out there ...

Lateef Hassan (12)

Wilson's School

Untitled

Billy jumped, Billy ducked. He couldn't dodge any longer. Billy wanted to stop dead. *Bring it on,* he thought to himself. There it was, it was coming right at him. *Boom!* The dodgeball hit him in the face …

'Billy, wake up!' He opened his eyes. Billy suddenly became awake.

Senthan Murugeswaran

Wilson's School

1941 Somewhere In France

Private Morse slowly advanced, his brain
struggling with the immense concentration,
his fingers frozen around the stock of his rifle,
anticipating artillery fire. Sudden whizzing
attracted his attention giving him a fraction of a
second to react.
'Incoming!' He screamed and then was blown into
the foxhole head first, dead.

Thomas Lovegrove (12)
Wilson's School

Jump

Ben charged up the stairs. A bullet hit the wall
above his head. He pushed the door open and
ran onto the roof. Ben stepped onto the edge and
turned around. His attacker sprinted through the
door and aimed his gun at Ben's trembling head.
Ben leapt off the roof …

Dominic Pellew (12)
Wilson's School

Sudden Attack

Shrill alarms, gunfire filled the air. The base was under attack. *Mr Oddjob is a fool,* I thought thinking he can take the base with 60 commandos and air support. He really is a fool.

My radio came alive, 'Sir, Section 4 has been compromised.'

'That's the reactor room.'

Boom!

Kieran Redmond (13)

Wilson's School

Untitled

I sprint with the ball to try line, nearly score, get tackled brutally. Damn! They get the ball, try to score. I tackle harder. Yeah! Ball still on the floor. It starts to grow legs; it turns into a zebra and runs. I tackle it! Man! It gets up...

Abisegan Sivakumar (12)

Wilson's School

Untitled

Early morning and a crazed driver. Jack's job was tough. He remembered it all, the bomb, the man, the pursuit. The man dived, Jack swerved. Impact. Both blew up but the man was on the loose, had a gun, a target and a reason. He's dangerous, he must be stopped!

Kash Pitan (12)

Wilson's School

Untitled

Sam slammed the accelerator down. He hit 150.
Soon enough the other driver veered away then
slammed into Sam's Bugatti. Sam lost control. His
car spun wildly. The car ripped and *boom!* Flames
burst into the air and Sam died whilst he was only
thinking about this beloved beautiful car.

Neeraj Radia (12)
Wilson's School

They're Close, They're Coming

Alex trudged over the cracked pathways and the slippery rubble. He stumbled over dead bodies but every time he got up, he heard the air raid siren blaring. He heard voices, marching gunfire. Germans, hundreds of them, tanks, armoured vehicles. They were coming closer. He crawled under a nearby body …

Matthew Hill (13)

Wilson's School

The Living Dead

Slowly and tentatively, Jack walked through the cemetery. He was starting to regret that stupid dare. As he was walking, he heard strange noises. Ignorantly thinking that it was the boys from school, Jack kept running. Suddenly, out of nowhere, Jack saw several different hands reaching out towards him …

Cecil Watson (12)

Wilson's School

Tiger Cave

Stu fell. Loud *crash!* Pitch-black, what to do? Run! Distant roar and Stu had to go. Dave dashed for the light. He roared ferociously! Where did he go? Stu stumbled to the exit. The cave lit up, another roar. *Crash!* Dave exploded on to Stu and tore him apart!

George O'Connor (13)

Wilson's School

The Captive Kid Of Holloway Close

James had a gun at his head, already loaded.
24 hours earlier James was going to his friend's
house to play when he was kidnapped. As James
fought back, the guy behind him fell down, dead.
A policeman came out from his hiding place, took
James back to his mum.

Luke Powell (13)
Wilson's School

The Power Of Silence

Ozzy crept down the alley. He could hear the howl of the wind as he approached the open field. He spied the shadows of the trees and sprinted to them. As Ozzy prowled the darkness he spotted a snack. The world went silent as the meal stopped still. Ozzy pounced …

Max Bruggy (12)
Wilson's School

Perception

Concealed in darkness behind a pillar, Alex reviewed his map of the palace. The golden monkey statue lay behind the last doors of the hallway. Unfortunately SWAT members armed with firearms guarded it loyally. He threw rubble into the darkness. The SWATs instinctively rotated to the noise before inspecting it.

Jake Field (13)

Wilson's School

Drop

' Wingspan of the plane …23 metres …resulted in loss of lift …' droned Mr Marston. *No one will ever fly,* thought Thomas. When will I need this information?

Twenty years later … Thomas ran towards the cliffs. Would the wings lift? His contraption rose. The machine shuddered and fell. The wing span? 23 metres.

Max Cobain (12)
Wilson's School

The Penalty Shoot Out

He stepped up to take the penalty. His heart was thumping at the speed of sound. This was what it all came down to. The seconds ticked on. He swiped his boot aiming for the bottom corner. He missed. After all he was Fernando Torres.

Daniel Fernandes (12)

Wilson's School

The Stranger

Trembling every step he takes. Pitch-black. A shadow lurks behind him. Who is it? He swerves to a narrow alleyway. Dead end. He looks back, a black cloak, black hat, black shoes. He closes his eyes and he can feel a cold bony hand. It's him, the living shadow …

Vignesh Nallathambi (12)
Wilson's School

The Meaning Of Life

It falls from the stratosphere. An endlessly
complex pattern of ice crystals, never to be
realised for it is one of untold quadrillions.
A diamond of the purest white and infinite
refraction of light. Striving to avoid heat and to
fulfil its sole purpose, settle. Please God let it
snow!

Archie Macgillivray (11)
Wilson's School

The Shark's Blood

The octopus slowly drifted in and out of the seaweed. The shark silently circled above its supposed prey. Suddenly it made its move and rocketed towards the octopus. However, the octopus had lightning-quick reactions and took the shark into its tentacles. The shark would never kill again.

James Sheridan (11)
Wilson's School

Flying Too Close To The Moon

It was Valentine's Day and James Nash had fallen in love. He believed he could fly and had special powers. Of course, he was human and did not have any powers. He wanted to give the moon to his love, so he jumped off the Empire State Building. He died.

Aravind Lakshminarayanan

Wilson's School

The Rat And The Cow

The rat and the cow were friends. One day there was a fundraising competition. The fundraising deadline was drawing close, so the rat stole to secure a win. The results were announced! The rat, who would have won comfortably, lost, because a raven saw the rat steal. The cow won!

Nathan Oluwadare (12)

Wilson's School

The Pointless Fight

There was one muffin left in the forest, the fight over it would be between the bear and the ant. The bear, seeing the ant was the other contestant immediately felt overconfident and was not trying his best. However the ant was cunning and beat the bear in the fight!

Jonathan D'Rozario (12)

Wilson's School

The Young Gosling

One day a mother goose and her goslings went for a swim. But one gosling went off on his own to explore. He couldn't find his way back, he was lost! He called for his mum for ages.
After a couple of minutes she found him and took him home.

Oliver De Carteret (13)
Wilson's School

The Foolish Rhino

The rhino barged through the elephants. He said,
'Ha, look at you weak losers!'
One of the baby elephants replied, 'Come on
then, I challenge you to a fight.'
'Pff, you couldn't beat me'
He charged head down and the elephant moved.
The rhino ran straight into a tree trunk.

Antony Evlogiev (12)
Wilson's School

285

Snowbell And The Presents

Every day, Snowbell counted her presents
beneath the tree. With one week until Christmas
she had 10 presents. She was very excited.
But that night a light exploded and her house
burned down, her presents; ruined. They were in
ashes the next day.
Don't count things before they are received.

Jacob Gartside (12)
Wilson's School

Fat Worm Slim

A very fat worm called Tom was always boasting
to his slim brother Tim about his strength. But
soon he paid the price. An enormous, keen-eyed
eagle swooped down from the sky. Slim Tim
managed to squeeze hastily through the fence to
safety, but poor fat Tom could not …

Robert Harwood (12)
Wilson's School

The Lame Dog

Once there was a lame dog.
One day the animals held a sporty event. The owl's team didn't encourage him because he was lame. The ox's team said, 'We haven't seen him run. Let's give him a chance.' The lame dog came first in his races, the owl's team lost.

Lok Sze Chung (12)
Wilson's School

The Fat Turkey Who Didn't Learn His Lesson

There was once a fat turkey. He always barged to the front to eat. But when Christmas came he was chosen to be eaten as he was nice and plump. When we hid he was too fat to hide and was chosen to be slaughtered. He hasn't been seen since!

Matthew Hyatt (12)
Wilson's School

289

The Pig And The Eggs

The fat pig with his basket of eggs thought to himself, *I will hatch these eggs into hens. These hens will lay eggs to buy sheep. By selling the wool from the sheep I will buy cows and sell their milk to become rich.* Alas, he dropped his eggs.

Fasihullah Muhammad (12)

Wilson's School

Lessons Learnt

There was a fox who bullied the other animals
continuously. The other animals decided to be
mean back to teach him a lesson. The fox grew
bad. The owl pitied him and told him to be nice.
The fox was, and the other animals were nice
back. Fox became happy.

James Nash (13)
Wilson's School

Decisions, Decisions

Roaming through the jungle, the lions were raging. The cat quickly jumped onto a tree. However the fox foolishly was deciding on which method to escape. Suddenly, he was slaughtered as the lions gobbled their prey. The cat disappeared into the dangerous depths of the jungle feeling very fortunate.

Mervin Nicholas (12)

Wilson's School

The Clearing

The wind was cold and my vision was obscured
by mist. Someone or something was watching
me. The whistling wind made the clearing seem
colder, then I spotted movement. A figure leapt
out as a sharp pain pierced my veins. I was
paralysed as the creature came for me again.

Patrick O'Connor (12)
Wilson's School

The Predator

I darted through the jungle wilderness into a clearing where I rested. The dense fog wrapped itself around me. I had to get out of this place. Far out. I spotted a black figure, *predator!* I scanned around for an exit. No way out! Looks like I'll be running, again!

Uzair Patel (13)

Wilson's School

The Lion And Jaguar Who Were Very Good Friends

The lion trod on a piece of glass from a bottle.
The jaguar, upon seeing this, pulled out the piece
of glass. The lion was grateful.
On the way home the jaguar fell onto a resting
buffalo. The lion, seeing this, defended the jaguar,
who was scared from the buffalo.

Shray Patel (12)
Wilson's School

295

The Terror

Slowly, silently, a crimson beast glided through the icy lagoon in search of prey. A flick of light and its attention was diverted to a puny seal. As swift as sound the daggonoth leaped out to her prey and slowly dragged it to the perilous caves down below, once again.

Christopher Sayanthan (12)
Wilson's School

The Peacock And The Cormorant

The peacock was beautiful but vain and selfish.
The cormorant was plain but kind and generous.
The peacock entered himself for a beauty
contest, while the cormorant's friends entered
him.
The judges spoke to the competitors and made
their decision. 'True beauty is in your heart,
therefore the cormorant wins.'

Thomas Short (12)
Wilson's School

The Gazelle And The Lion

Once not so long ago, lived Gazelle. He inhabited
the vast plains of Africa, along with many other
creatures. Gazelle believed that he was the fastest
of the animals, but he was getting cocky.
One day Gazelle angered Lion and tried to flee
him, but Lion caught and killed Gazelle.

Harry Rogers (13)
Wilson's School

A Nutty Ending

A selfish squirrel once lived; he was the best nut
collector of all time. He was so good there were
no more nuts for the other squirrels.
During winter most squirrels died of starvation
but the selfish squirrel did not spare any. Alas his
tree fell down with a thump.

Amir Quadir (13)
Wilson's School

299

The Turtle And The Owl

Once there was a turtle and an owl who lived
in a big forest. They were both friends and the
turtle depended on the owl to catch its food.
Unfortunately the owl had to go on holiday and
the turtle was left without food, and the turtle
died.

Aneesh Gupta (12)
Wilson's School

300

Information

We hope you have enjoyed reading this book - and that you will continue to enjoy it in the coming years.

If you like reading and writing, drop us a line or give us a call and we'll send you a free information pack. Alternatively visit our website at
www.youngwriters.co.uk

Write to:

Young Writers Information,
Remus House,
Coltsfoot Drive,
Peterborough,
PE2 9JX

Tel: (01733) 890066
Email: youngwriters@forwardpress.co.uk